Maestro Von Haughty

PRESENTS

One Dark
and
Dreadful
Night

Randy Cecil

A Wayward Orphans Production

Henry Holt and Company

This book owes a great deal to Joe Shlichta,
and also to Reka, Martha, and Laura.
Thank you! —R. C.

Henry Holt and Company, LLC
Publishers since 1866
115 West 18th Street
New York, New York 10011
www.henryholt.com

Henry Holt is a registered trademark of Henry Holt and Company, LLC
Copyright © 2004 by Randy Cecil
All rights reserved.
Distributed in Canada by H. B. Fenn and Company Ltd.

Library of Congress Cataloging-in-Publication Data
Cecil, Randy.
One dark and dreadful night / Randy Cecil.
Summary: Maestro Von Haughty wants to present three thrilling tales of terror and misfortune, but
members of the Wayward Orphans Theatre make some very silly changes to the costumes and script.
[1. Theater—Fiction. 2. Orphans—Fiction. 3. Humorous stories.] I. Title.
PZ7.C2999On 2004   [E]—dc22   2003023015

ISBN 0-8050-6779-5 / EAN 978-0-8050-6779-8
First Edition—2004
Printed in the United States of America on acid-free paper. ∞
1 3 5 7 9 10 8 6 4 2

The artist used oil paint on Aquarelle Arches paper to create the illustrations for this book.

Good evening . . .

and welcome to the Wayward Orphans
Theatre. I am Maestro Von Haughty.
   Tonight I am proud to present three
tales of terror and misfortune. We begin
with Little Red Rose in the very tragic
tale of . . .

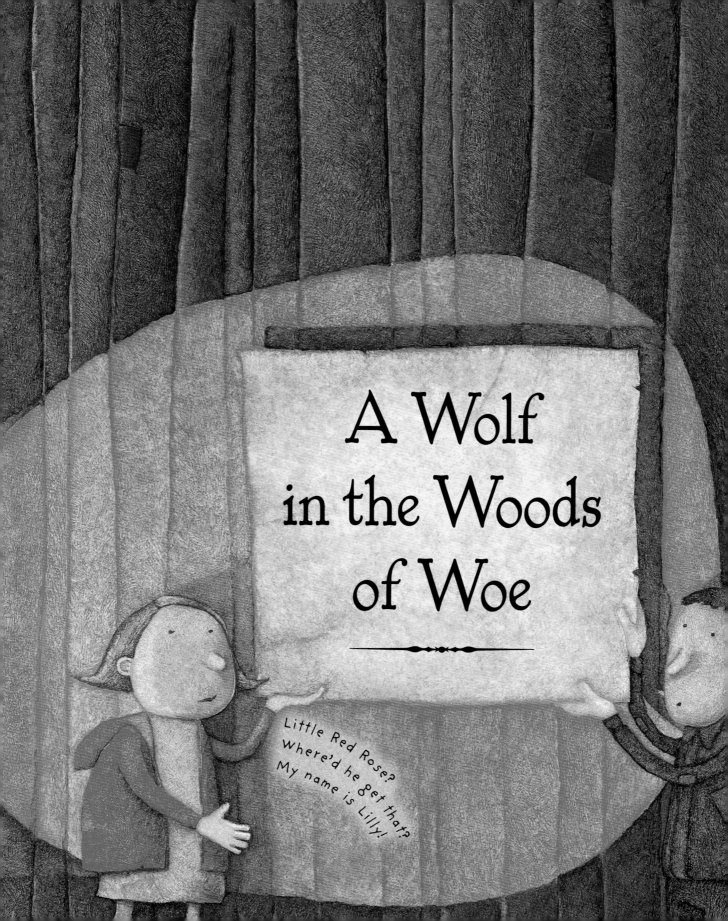

A Wolf in the Woods of Woe

Little Red Rose?
Where'd he get that?
My name is Lilly!

Once upon a time, there was a poor peasant child named Lilly Riley-Hood.

Being a poor peasant child, Lilly had very little to call her own. Her only possession was a pretty red coat given to her by her beloved grandmother.

Do you think we can talk wardrobe into doing something about this outfit?

One dark and dreadful night, young Lilly's mother came to her and said, "My dear little Lilly, bring this cake to your grandmother. She has fallen ill, and it will do her good. But take care to stay on the trail as you pass through the Woods of Woe, for there is a ferocious wolf lurking about."

Hey! These shoes are full of holes! Do you always treat your poor peasants like this?

The hapless child went into the Woods of Woe, where the dark grew darker, and the trees grew more twisted, and all the sharp pointy things grew sharper and pointier.

Hmm. The briars and brambles grew sharper and pointier.

The path was so twisted and overgrown that the thorny branches snagged and tore at Lilly's pretty red coat.

But this was not what worried Lilly. What worried her was the shadowy presence that seemed to be following her. Lilly clutched the cake plate in fear. Suddenly out from behind a gnarled tree pounced . . .

I think somebody has gone a little overboard with the briars and brambles.

. . . the wolf!

Aaaarrrghhh!

Aaagh!

Aaagh!

Aaagh!

In a suit?

Anyway, he was ferocious! Slobber dripped from his
teeth as he flashed a grotesque smile! His razor-sharp
claws slashed through the night air!

Hold it!
I don't think
I like the way
this story is going.
Being a poor peasant child is the pits.
And I am definitely NOT going
to be eaten by this wolf!
Hey!
Oh dear!

I want to be a princess!

A fairy princess with wings!

Oh, woe is me!

Butterflies?! No! No! No!
Stop it right this minute!
This is MY production!

No more nonsense!

That is enough!

I am going to start a
new story, and I want
NO interruptions!
No butterflies, no
kittens, and especially
no fairy princess!
Is that understood?

All right, then,
let's begin . . .

The Beans
of Doom

Once upon a time, there was a boy named Jack, who lived with his mother and a cow in a little tiny cottage. They were desperately poor, and Jack's mother was ill with fever and ague.

A-goo? What's a-goo?

One dark and dreadful night, Jack's mother
sent him to market to sell the cow. But on the
way, Jack met a mysterious stranger who offered
him three magic beans in exchange for the
cow. Jack thought this was a pretty good deal.
After all, how often does one come across
magic beans?

When Jack returned home with only
three beans, his mother flew into a frenzy.
She was so blind with fever that she didn't
see the magic in the beans, and threw them
as far as she could. Because she was weak
with ague, this was not very far.

By morning, as you might have guessed already, the beans had grown into an enormous bean stalk that stretched high into the clouds.

"FEE, FIE, FOE, FUM!" boomed the voice of a horrible, gruesome, giant . . .

... bunny?!?

There are no giant bunnies in this story! Giant bunnies aren't gruesome or scary! There is no drama in oversized rabbits!

Excuse me. I would like to apologize for all the nonsense that you have so kindly put up with so far. This is not at all what I had intended.

Why don't we start the last tale now? No fairy princess, no cows or butterflies, and definitely NO giant bunnies!

So, without further ado, I give you . . .

Once upon a time, there lived a very poor family named the Glumms. They lived in a teeny cottage at the edge of Foggy Forest. Now let's get straight to the disastrous events! Mrs. Glumm had hatched an awful scheme:

"Take the children and leave them deep in Foggy Forest!"

Excuse me, we can hear you!

So one dark and dreadful night, Mr. Glumm led his children away. As the fog grew thicker . . .

AAAGH! I said no giant rabbits! And no fairy princess! Bring those kids back! This story is not finished yet! Do you hear me? BRING THEM BACK!

THAT DOES IT!

This is the END! This dark and dreadful production is OVER!

A Western with a giant bunny and kittens and butterflies!